Good Luck, Anna Hibiscus!

Good Luck, ANNA HIBISCUS!

by Atinuke

Illustrated by Lauren Tobia

Kane Miller

A DIVISION OF EDC PUBLISHING

First American Edition 2011
Kane Miller, A Division of EDC Publishing

First published in 2009 by Walker Books Ltd., London (England)
Text © 2009 Atinuke
Illustrations © 2009 Lauren Tobia

For information contact:
Kane Miller, A Division of EDC Publishing
P.O. Box 470663
Tulsa, OK 74147-0663
www.kanemiller.com
www.edcpub.com
www.usbornebooksandmore.com

Library of Congress Control Number: 2010934455

Printed and bound in the United States of America
7 8 9 10 11 12 13 14 15 16
ISBN: 978-1-61067-785-1

To Tiger Malachi Oluwalase and
Noa Caradog Babatunde. Love you.

A.

To Lizzie and Alice
from their proud Mum

L.T.

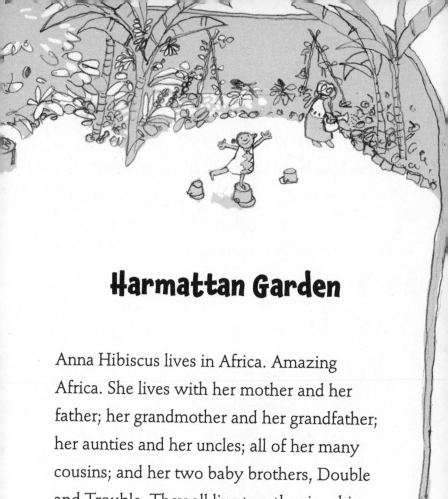

Harmattan Garden

Anna Hibiscus lives in Africa. Amazing Africa. She lives with her mother and her father; her grandmother and her grandfather; her aunties and her uncles; all of her many cousins; and her two baby brothers, Double and Trouble. They all live together in a big white house in the middle of a bright and beautiful garden!

Anna Hibiscus loves the green of their
garden. She loves the red and the yellow
flowers that grow in the cool grass. She
loves the leafy trees and their big, bright
fruit. She loves the birds that sing in the
branches, and the lizards that run
along the roots.

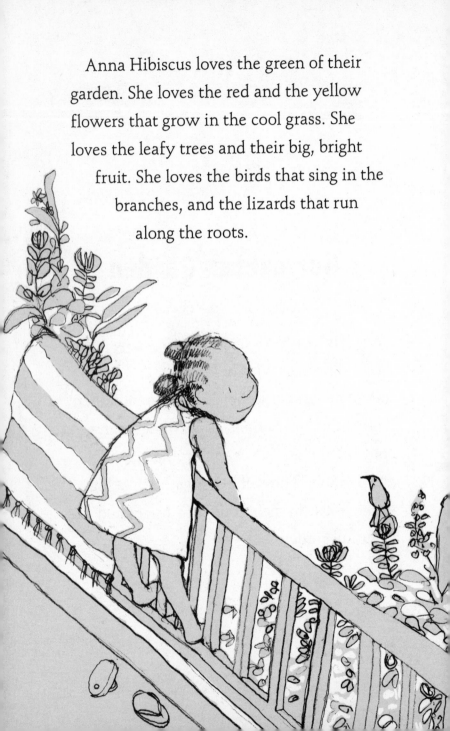

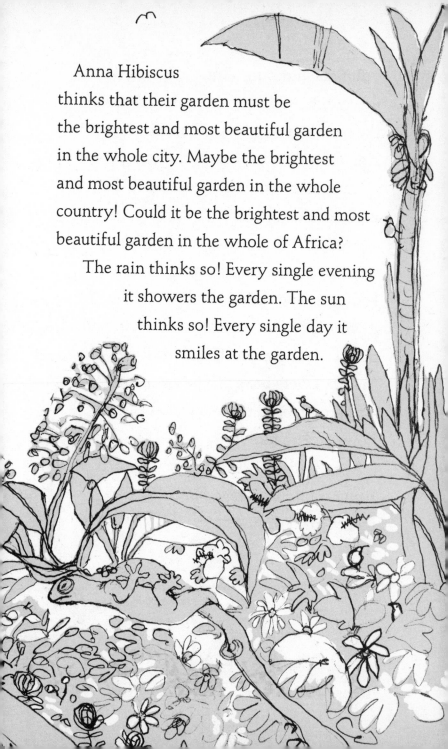

Anna Hibiscus
thinks that their garden must be
the brightest and most beautiful garden
in the whole city. Maybe the brightest
and most beautiful garden in the whole
country! Could it be the brightest and most
beautiful garden in the whole of Africa?

The rain thinks so! Every single evening
it showers the garden. The sun
thinks so! Every single day it
smiles at the garden.

But one morning, Anna Hibiscus woke
up, and the sun was not smiling through
the bedroom window. "Where is the sun?"
Anna asked, in her croaky, morning voice.

Chocolate and Angel woke up. "The sun
is gone!" Angel cried.

Anna and Chocolate and Angel ran to the
window to see. Angel was right: The sun
had gone, and the sky was not bright blue;
it was cloudy brown! Anna Hibiscus looked
down at the garden. The green leaves of
the trees were brown. The green grass
was brown. The red and yellow
flowers were brown.

"The garden is dead!"
Anna Hibiscus opened her
mouth and cried.

Chocolate and Angel joined her in crying. Louder and louder they cried. Clarity and Joy, the big girl cousins, rushed into the bedroom.

"Way-tin happen?" they shouted.

Anna Hibiscus and Angel and Chocolate were crying too loud to speak. They pointed up to the hazy brown sky. They pointed down to the dusty brown garden. Clarity and Joy smiled and laughed and dried their small cousins' tears.

"It's harmattan time!" Clarity said.

"You no remember?" asked Joy. "Every year is de same thing. One harmattan wind blows over Sahara Desert. It blows de desert sand all the way down to our own country."

"An' dat same sand is now covering the sky and the garden," said Clarity. "The sun is not gone; it is only the sand that is covering it."

"Will the rain wash the sand off our garden?" sobbed Anna.

"No-o," said Clarity. "For the next four months we will have no rain, only dusty sand and wind. After dat the rain go fall, the sand go finish, and the sun will shine again."

"But before that," announced Joy, "Christmas!"

Anna Hibiscus and Chocolate and Angel stopped crying. Christmas! Now they remembered the harmattan. It was always dry and dusty at Christmas time.

Suddenly Anna Hibiscus was happy.
Happy and excited. Because when
Christmas came she was going to Canada
to play in the snow!

Anna Hibiscus ran into her parents' room.
Double and Trouble were standing up in
their cot looking towards the window.

"Christmas!" shouted Anna Hibiscus,
clapping her hands. Double Trouble smiled
and clapped their hands too. Clapping was
their new best thing.

Anna went to stand by their cot. She
looked out of the window. "But before
Christmas," she sighed,
"harmattan." No sun and
no rain. Only dry, dusty
sand.

Luckily for Anna Hibiscus's family, there was a good well in the garden of the big white house. A good well full of clear, cold water. In the dry and thirsty harmattan months the water was low. But it never ran dry.

Every dry day Anna Hibiscus drank all the clear, cold water that she wanted. And every dusty, hot evening she was given one bucket of water to wash with.

"One bucket is already a lot of water," said Grandmother. "Be careful."

"When I was small, every harmattan our well dry up," said Grandfather. "We were grateful for one cup of water to wash ourselves."

Everybody in the big white house was careful. And everybody was grateful. More than this, everybody tried to leave some water in their bucket.

Double and Trouble got half a bucket each. The water came up to their necks. Double Trouble sat for a long time in their buckets. It was the only time they were cool. It was the only time they were quiet!

15

Anna Hibiscus stood in the bath with her bucket of water. She poured one big, cool, jug of water over her hot and dusty self. Ohhhh! She wanted to pour more, but she stopped. She soaped and then carefully rinsed herself with one and a half jugfuls of water. She was clean! And there was almost half of the cool water left! Anna Hibiscus got out of the bath. She was hot again already!

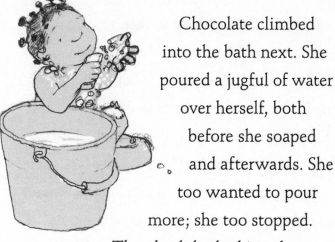

Chocolate climbed into the bath next. She poured a jugful of water over herself, both before she soaped and afterwards. She too wanted to pour more; she too stopped. They both looked into her bucket. There was half left!

Now it was Angel's turn. Angel splashed cool jugfuls of water over herself one after another. More and more she poured. Ohhhh! Now she was not only clean; she was cool. Angel looked into her bucket. All the water was gone!

Anna and Chocolate looked at Angel.

"Come out! Come out!" Benz and Wonderful, their big boy cousins, banged on the door. "Grandfather is waiting for you!"

"Hurry up! Hurry up!" shouted Clarity and Common Sense. "You are the last ones!"

Anna Hibiscus and Chocolate and Angel quickly carried their buckets to the tank in the garden where the well water was stored. Grandmother and Grandfather, aunties and uncles and cousins were waiting. Carefully Anna and Chocolate tipped the water left in their buckets into the tank.

"Good girl," everybody said to Anna Hibiscus.

"Well done," they said to Chocolate.

Angel started to cry. Grandfather looked into her bucket. It was empty.

"Don' cry," he said. "Tomorrow you can try harder. And you will do better."

Then Grandfather nodded at the grown-up cousins. Sociable ran to the water tank and grabbed the handle of the pump. Thank God picked up a long hose, and when Grandfather nodded again Sociable began to pump. Thank God pointed the hose at the mango trees. The whole family held their breath. A stream of clear water sprayed out of the end of the hose. The mango trees were green again!

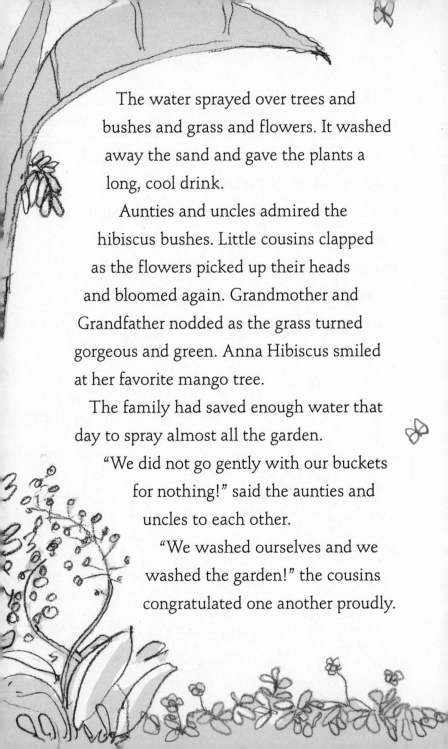

The water sprayed over trees and bushes and grass and flowers. It washed away the sand and gave the plants a long, cool drink.

Aunties and uncles admired the hibiscus bushes. Little cousins clapped as the flowers picked up their heads and bloomed again. Grandmother and Grandfather nodded as the grass turned gorgeous and green. Anna Hibiscus smiled at her favorite mango tree.

The family had saved enough water that day to spray almost all the garden.

"We did not go gently with our buckets for nothing!" said the aunties and uncles to each other.

"We washed ourselves and we washed the garden!" the cousins congratulated one another proudly.

And this, thought Anna Hibiscus, is why our garden is the brightest and most beautiful garden in the whole country!

Everybody walked around the garden. Anna went to look at the flowers growing by the gate. Through the gate she saw the girls who sold oranges and plantains to make money for their families. The girls were going home for the night. Anna Hibiscus smiled and waved.

"Look!" she shouted, pointing at the flowers."

The girls looked at Anna Hibiscus. But they did not smile at her. They did not wave. They frowned. Anna was confused.

"Bedtime, Anna," her mother called, and Anna Hibiscus turned away from the gate.

But she continued to worry. Why did the gate girls not wave and smile at her?

The next morning Anna Hibiscus ran down to the gate. The air was already hot and dry; the garden was already dusty. The gate girls were there, waiting for early morning customers.

Anna Hibiscus shouted, "Good morning, Angelina! Good morning, Concertina! Good morning, Ngosi!"

The gate girls looked at Anna Hibiscus. They did not smile. They did not say good morning.

"Way-tin happen?" Anna asked. "Wha's wrong?"

The girls did not answer. They just carried on with their work.

Anna Hibiscus saw that their clothes were stained. Their faces were shiny with sweat, and their arms and legs were dirty.

Maybe they did not even have one cup of water to wash with like Grandfather did, she thought.

The gate girls looked around and saw Anna Hibiscus still waiting there.

"Le' me tell you, Anna Hibiscus," said Angelina, sounding angry. "Then you can go. There is no more water in this useless ye-ye city."

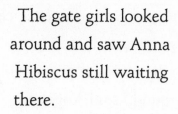

"No more water?" asked Anna Hibiscus, thinking of her family's well.

"Poor person water finish," snapped Concertina. "Well dry. Tap no run at-all at-all."

"Old people, small brothers and sisters suffer and die now," said Ngosi.

The gate girls stopped speaking. Anna Hibiscus started to cry.

"In dis your compound you throw water for ground," said Angelina.

The gate girls turned their backs on Anna Hibiscus and went back to their work. They had no time to cry.

Anna Hibiscus no longer wondered why they were not her friends. "I did not know!" she shouted.

Anna ran to Grandmother and Grandfather on the veranda. She told them about the gate girls, and about the poor, thirsty children in the city.

Grandfather and Grandmother looked serious. They ordered Thank God to pump water and Sociable to carry it to the gate for the poor girls and their families.

Then they summoned everybody in the big white house out onto the veranda.

"Is this true?" Grandmother and Grandfather asked the uncles and aunties. "Poor people are suffering in the city?"

The aunties and uncles looked surprised. "It is true that the wells are dry, and water has become costly," they said.

"Go and ask the gate girls," sobbed Anna. "People in the city are suffering."

"It is true," said Sociable.

Grandmother and Grandfather and Anna's mother and father and all the aunties and uncles and cousins and Anna herself sat silent.

"My mango tree is not suffering," Anna Hibiscus said.

Everybody nodded.

"Because we save water for it every day," said Sweetheart, the smallest girl cousin.

"That is why the whole garden is growing green and lovely." Anna's mother smiled.

"But outside in the city," Anna went on, "children are not growing lovely. They are suffering because nobody saves them any water."

Angel and Sweetheart started to cry.

"Anna Hibiscus, what can we do?" said her father. "We do not have enough water for the whole city."

"We never even had enough water for the whole garden," said Uncle Tunde.

"Did we let that stop us?" said Anna's mother.

"No!" cried Auntie Grace and Auntie Joly and Clarity and Common Sense and Joy

and Benz and Wonderful and Angel and
Chocolate and Sweetheart and Anna.

"We might have enough water for the
children of the city," said Uncle Bizi Sunday.

"Let us try," said Anna's father, sighing.

"Agreed!" shouted Anna and all of her
cousins.

"So we have decided!" said Grandmother,
smiling.

Double and Trouble clapped their hands.

"Every spare ounce of water, let us
put it in the tank," said
Grandfather.

"Then we can water
the children of the
city!" shouted
Anna.

And so it was that Anna Hibiscus's garden became an ordinary garden. The grass disappeared. The flowers died. The bushes wilted. The trees were dry and dusty all harmattan long. It was no longer the brightest and most beautiful garden in the whole city.

But outside the gate a line of hopeful children grew with their cups and bottles, red and yellow and green and blue. When Sociable filled them up with water, their smiles were the brightest and most beautiful smiles in the whole city. The brightest and most beautiful smiles in the whole country.

28

And Anna Hibiscus and Chocolate and even Angel learned to wash using only one jugful of water.

"In order to see the most beautiful smiles in the whole world!" Anna Hibiscus said.

31

Double Trouble for Anna Hibiscus

Anna Hibiscus lives in Africa. Amazing Africa. She lives with her whole family: her mother and her father; her grandmother and her grandfather; her uncles and their wives; her aunties and their husbands; all of her cousins; and her own two brothers, Double and Trouble.

Double and Trouble are boys. Double and Trouble are babies. Double and Trouble are twins. That means Trouble. Double Trouble.

One harmattan afternoon all of Anna's
family were in the garden. Everybody was
hot. Grandmother and Grandfather were
on the veranda. Small cousins lay on the
ground where the grass was gone. Aunties
and uncles sat in the shade of wilted bushes.
Big cousins were up in branches among
the sagging, dusty leaves. Everybody was
too hot to move. Everybody was too hot to
speak.

34

Everybody except
for Double Trouble.
Double and Trouble
were crawling around the
garden as fast as they could,
shouting, "Koko! Koko! Koko!" They
were chasing Koko the parrot. They wanted
to pull his pretty feathers. Everybody loved
Koko's feathers, but nobody had one.

"Koko! Koko! Koko!" Double Trouble
shouted loud.

Koko flew from tree to
tree. He always landed
high up, where Double
and Trouble could not reach
him. But still it annoyed
him when Double
Trouble sat underneath
his branch shouting
and crying, "Koko!
Koko! Koko!"

All the shouting was beginning to give
everybody a big headache. But everybody
was too hot to move. Everybody was
too hot to speak.

"Shhh," Miracle said.
"If you are good
I will draw you a
picture."
She drew a parrot in
the dust.
"Koko! Koko! Koko!"
Trouble shouted.

Uncle Tunde said,
"Trouble, come here! If
you are quiet I will carry
you on my shoulders."

Trouble sat on Uncle
Tunde's shoulders
shouting, "Koko!
Koko! Koko!"

"Stop," said Anna Hibiscus, "and I will sing you a song."

But Double and Trouble wanted to sing too. "Koko! Koko! Koko!" they sang loudly.

Auntie Joly called out, "Double! Trouble! If you are quiet, then you can have a sweet!"

All the cousins looked at Auntie Joly. She looked back at them.

"You can all have one," she said, "tonight – after food."

Double and Trouble sat on Auntie Joly's lap, their teeth glued together with sweets, shouting, "Dodo! Dodo! Dodo!"

Suddenly it was not only Koko who was annoyed. Grandfather was annoyed too.

"Oya! Siesta time!" he announced.

The whole family heaved a sigh of relief. Siesta meant they could all go inside to their bedrooms. Turn on their cold air conditioners. Lie down on their cool, soft beds and close their hot, dusty eyes.

Everybody was happy. Everybody except for Double and Trouble. Anna Hibiscus's mother and father carried them kicking and screaming to their cot.

"Koko! Koko! Koko!" they shouted.

Double and Trouble continued shouting in their cot while their mother and father pretended to be asleep. They knew if they kept still and quiet, Double Trouble would soon go to sleep too.

"Koko! Koko! Koko!" screamed Double Trouble.

Anna Hibiscus
and Chocolate
and Angel were
in their bedroom
next door. They
were trying to
sleep.

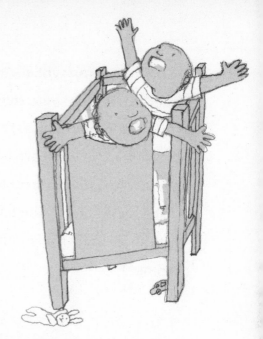

"Be quiet,
Double!" shouted
Anna.

"Be quiet, Trouble!" shouted Chocolate.

"We are trying to sleep!" shouted Angel.

Benz and Wonderful were in the room
next to the girls. The girls' shouting woke
them up, and they started to jump on their
beds and fight.

Clarity and Joy and Common Sense
shared the other room next to the boys.

"Stop fighting!" they shouted, loud and
cross. "We are trying to sleep."

Their shouting woke Miracle and Sweetheart, who were sleeping with Auntie Joly in the room next to the big girls. Miracle and Sweetheart started to cry, and Auntie Joly had to get up to comfort them.

"Shh! Shh! Shh!" She patted them crossly. "Stop shouting!" she shouted at the big girl cousins.

Then she banged on the boys' door. "You carry on, and I will send you to Grandfather!" she shouted.

"Be quiet!" she called to Anna and Chocolate and Angel. "Why are you making so much noise?"

"Koko! Koko! Koko! Koko! Koko!" Double and Trouble screamed. That was the answer!

Auntie Joly knocked on the door of Anna Hibiscus's parents' bedroom. "Sister! Brother! Your babies-o. They are disturbing everybody-o."

By now Auntie Joly had woken up the uncles.

"Can't you let a man sleep in peace?" they shouted loudly.

Grandmother and Grandfather came upstairs. They went into Anna Hibiscus's parents' room. In the middle of all that noise, Anna's parents were fast asleep and snoring next to the cot. Grandmother and Grandfather picked Double Trouble up under one arm each. Then they went back downstairs to where they took their siesta on a mat under a slow, whirring fan.

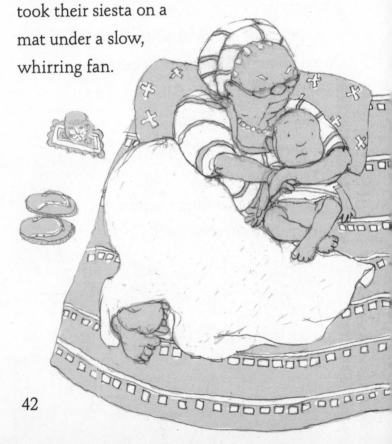

Double and Trouble tried to shout, but
Grandmother and Grandfather looked them
in the eye. They tried to wriggle away,
but Grandmother and Grandfather pinned
them down with their strong, old arms. So
Double and Trouble went to sleep.

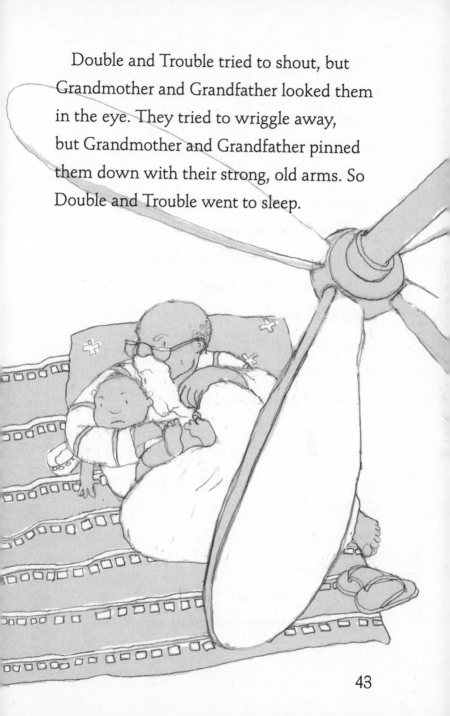

For two whole minutes everybody in
the big white house was fast asleep. Then
Grandmother snored and Grandfather's
body jolted.

Double and Trouble woke up.

"Koko," whispered Double.

"Koko," Trouble agreed.

They crawled across the floor
to the screen door. They
tried hard to open
that door. First they
tried to push it, but
that did not work.

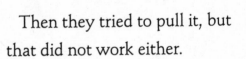

Then they tried to pull it, but
that did not work either.

They tried
to reach the
handle, but
they were too small.

44

They tried to move
a chair to reach the
handle, but it was too
heavy.

Finally Trouble
climbed onto Double's
back. At last! He
could reach the handle.
Trouble pulled. The door
slid open. Trouble slid
with the door, off Double's
back, and onto the floor.

Double crawled straight out through the
open door and into the garden.
Trouble followed him.
"Koko! Koko! Koko!"
they shouted.

Koko was sitting in a mango tree taking his siesta. He opened his eyes and looked down at Double Trouble. He closed his eyes again. They could not reach him up here.

Double Trouble looked up at Koko. Then Trouble looked at Double. Trouble climbed onto Double's back. He tried to stand up. He stretched up to the branch. He fell off.

Then he saw the sweet jar. Oh! Sweeties! Sweeties were better than parrots.

Double Trouble worked hard to get the lid off that sweet jar. They tried sucking it. No good. They tried biting it. Ow, hard. They tried shaking it and tipping it upside down and pulling it. Then by chance they turned it. The lid came off.

Double Trouble settled down quietly to eat the sweets. They worked hard at it. They ate them with the wrappers on; they ate them with the wrappers off. They ate them one, two, three, four, five at a time.

They snatched them from each other,
wiping their sticky hands on each other's
faces and in each other's hair.

Koko woke up. All was quiet under the tree. He opened his eyes and looked down. He squawked. Double Trouble were gone, and in their place were two monsters. Two masquerade men. Small ones, but scary. Koko flew up out of the tree. He flew around and around the house, sounding the alarm the only way he could, by squawking, "Koko! Koko! Koko!"

Nobody in the house woke up. Nobody except for Anna Hibiscus. She had been dreaming that Double and Trouble were still making noise. "I am trying to sleep!" she shouted. And sat up.

Now she could hear better. It was Koko making noise! Anna got up and looked out of the window. Koko was flying around and around the house. What was wrong?

Anna Hibiscus went downstairs. She
tiptoed past Grandmother and Grandfather
and went out through the open door. There
were Double and Trouble. They were eating
all the sweets from the sweet jar. Anna ran
to take it away from them.

"Stop!"

Anna Hibiscus shouted,
in her loudest voice.

Anna Hibiscus's shout
woke up everybody in
the big white house.
Wha's dat? they all
thought. Wha's going on?

Anna Hibiscus grabbed the sweet jar and tried to pull it away from Double Trouble.

Double Trouble held on to the jar. They were not going to let go. Never. Anna Hibiscus let go of the jar and tried to pull Double Trouble off instead. They were so sticky. Anna Hibiscus got covered in sticky sweet wrappers too.

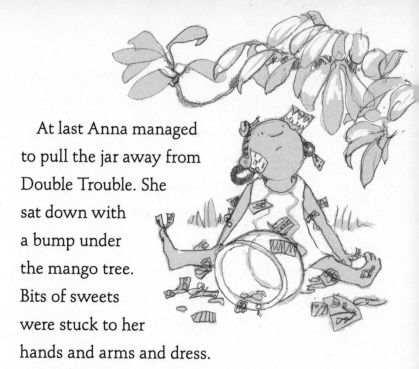

At last Anna managed
to pull the jar away from
Double Trouble. She
sat down with
a bump under
the mango tree.
Bits of sweets
were stuck to her
hands and arms and dress.

Anna Hibiscus's mother and father
and aunties and uncles and cousins came
running out into the garden to see what all
the noise was about. Only Grandmother
and Grandfather were still sleeping.

"Anna Hibiscus!" her mother gasped.

"What have you done?" said Auntie Joly.

"The sweets!" Angel cried.

"All gone!" wailed Wonderful.

Anna Hibiscus pointed. But Double Trouble had gone too. They had crawled away after Koko, leaving Anna alone with the empty jar and everybody looking at her.

"It was not me," she said. "It was Double Trouble."

"Anna Hibiscus!" said her mother again.

"Double and Trouble are sleeping in their cot," said her father. He had been asleep

when Grandmother and Grandfather had
taken them out.

"You are telling lies," said Auntie Joly,
shaking her head.

"And blaming other people," said Uncle
Tunde, looking stern.

"It's not true!" said Anna, bursting into
tears.

But everybody looked at her sticky fingers
and arms and the wrappers stuck to her
dress, and everybody was stern
and sad. Anna Hibiscus was
sent to her room.

Then Grandmother and Grandfather
woke up and were told the whole story.

"Double Trouble are not in their cot!" they
said. "We brought them down here to sleep
with us."

"Then where are they?" asked Anna's
mother.

"They are here!" shouted Benz.

And there they were, two little
masquerade men, lying under a bush
holding on to their stomachs and feeling
very sick.

"Anna Hibiscus is
not sick," said Miracle.

"No," agreed Clarity. "And
she does not have a red mouth."

"Or a purple one," noticed Chocolate.

"She did not even have a sticky mouth,"
said Uncle Tunde.

"Only sticky hands and dress," wondered
Anna's mother.

"Which does not prove that she was
the one eating sweets," said Grandmother
firmly.

Anna Hibiscus was called back downstairs. She explained how she had tried to pull the jar away from Double Trouble and then tried to pull Double Trouble away from the jar.

"That's why I am so sticky with sweets." Anna Hibiscus wept.

"Oh, Anna Hibiscus! Sorry-o. Sorry!" everybody said.

"Just because it looks like somebody has done something ..." said Grandfather.

"... it does not mean they did it," said Grandmother. "That is why we assume people are innocent."

Grandmother and Grandfather looked sternly at everybody just as everybody had looked sternly at Anna Hibiscus. Everybody said sorry again.

"Is OK," said Anna. But she did not smile. She went outside and climbed into the mango tree. She did not feel like being with anybody.

Then Koko the
parrot flew into the tree.
He landed on the branch
right above Anna. He
flapped his wings, and his
most beautiful feather fell
into Anna's lap.

Anna sat still, staring at the feather. Then she smiled her biggest smile and shouted, "Everybody! Come and look at this!"

Anna Hibiscus's New Clothes

Anna Hibiscus lives in Africa. Amazing Africa. Hot Africa. Dry Africa. But soon, very soon, Anna Hibiscus will fly in an airplane over land and over seas to visit Granny Canada, her mother's mother. Yes, Anna Hibiscus is going to Canada. Cold Canada.

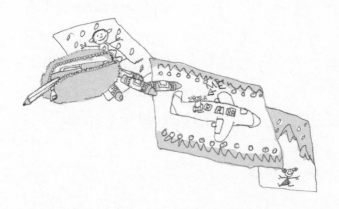

Anna was wondering about cold when her mother came into her room.

"Anna Hibiscus, it is time to sort you out for Canada. You will need warm clothes for the cold."

Anna Hibiscus looked in her cupboard. There were bubas and wrappas. She was not sure that anybody wore bubas and wrappas in Canada. There were strappy dresses. But they were for hot weather.

Anna spotted two dresses Auntie Comfort had sent her from America. They both had long sleeves and one even had a petticoat. Anna Hibiscus took them out. She was not going to be cold in Canada!

Anna Hibiscus's mother looked at the cotton dresses. She looked in the cupboard. She went to find Anna Hibiscus's father.

"Anna Hibiscus has nothing warm to wear in Canada," she said. "What are we going to do?"

"Don't worry; we'll find something," he said.

Grandmother and Grandfather and the aunties and uncles and cousins were called to look for warm clothes for Anna Hibiscus.

Everybody in the big white house joined in the search. Boxes and bags were pulled out from under beds and off the tops of cupboards. Clothes stuffed into the bottoms of wardrobes were shaken out and examined.

"That is no good!" her mother said.

"WARM! WARM!" Uncle Tunde shouted to Auntie Grace.

"Don't touch my bottom box!" Joy shouted at Sweetheart. "Those clothes are all too big for Anna Hibiscus anyway!"

Auntie Joly said to Miracle, "Look! It fits you! Too small for Anna Hibiscus."

"How cold can it be in Canada?" Grandmother shouted, when Grandfather held up a long, woolen scarf. "Do you want to suffocate the child?"

Anna Hibiscus was glad everybody was finding clothes for her, but in the end, after everybody had finished looking and shouting, there were only two long-sleeved, cotton dresses laid out on Anna Hibiscus's bed. Grandfather's old scarf (from the time he had fallen into the lagoon and caught a cold), two undershirts which were too small for Wonderful, and some long gray socks which the aunties used to wear at school.

Anna Hibiscus looked at the boys' undershirts and Grandfather's scarf and the old gray school socks and her two dresses. She had a miserable feeling.

Anna Hibiscus's mother noticed that miserable feeling. She had it too. "Anna Hibiscus cannot go to Canada looking like that!" she said. "I will phone Granny—"

"No, no!" Grandmother said. "Don' bother your mother."

"She will think we cannot look after Anna Hibiscus well-well," said Grandfather. "We have plenty of good, warm clothes here in Africa."

"Where?" Anna asked.

Grandfather looked at Grandmother. Grandmother looked at the aunties. The aunties looked at each other.

"I know where there are some new shops selling oyinbo clothes," Clarity said.

Grandmother frowned.

"What is 'oyinbo'?" Sweetheart asked.

"Somebody like my mother," whispered Anna Hibiscus. "Somebody with white skin, from abroad."

"They are good, warm clothes," Joy said.

"Just right for the cold Canadian winter!" added Common Sense.

"You see!" said Grandfather.

Joy, Clarity and Common Sense got ready to take Anna Hibiscus shopping. They wore their going-out shoes, their tight, cross-no-gutter skirts and their party blouses.

Anna Hibiscus was excited. She was going out with the big girl cousins – alone. Maybe she would get big girls' clothes too!

Grandmother looked hard at them when they came downstairs.

"I don' want you coming back with clothes that are not suitable for Anna Hibiscus," she said. She tied her wrappa tighter and looked around for her handbag. "I will come with you."

"Grandmother!" said Clarity. "The shops are far. The roads are rough."

"The buses are crowded and shake the body up and down, up and down," said Joy.

"Shopping in the harmattan heat blows the feet up like balloons!" Common Sense added.

Grandmother looked even harder at them. "Don' tell me what I already know!" she said sharply. "Somebody needs to keep an eye on you."

"I will keep an eye on them," Uncle Tunde volunteered.

"Good," said Grandmother. "Then you can take us all in your car. After the girls have changed back into their wrappas."

So Grandmother and Anna Hibiscus and Clarity and Common Sense and Joy (in bubbas and wrappers), together with Benz and Wonderful (who came to look after the car while they were off shopping) and Auntie Joly (who wanted to be dropped off on the way), all squeezed themselves into Uncle Tunde's car, and off they drove.

It took a long, hot, bumpy time to get to the shops. When they finally arrived they were all hot and sweating.

The shops were big and fine with sparkling windows showing off expensive oyinbo outfits.

Grandmother took a deep breath, adjusted her headtie, and headed towards the first shop. Uncle Tunde, Joy, Clarity, Common Sense and Anna Hibiscus followed.

Inside the shop it was quiet and cold. Grandmother shivered. They looked around for the trader, but they did not see anybody. All Anna could see were rows of clothes with printed labels.

"Where is the shop trader?" Grandmother asked. "Why is she not here to do business with us? Does she not want to sell her clothes? Anybody could be carrying them away!"

At the sound of her voice, a young man with a long, scrawny neck and very shiny oyinbo clothes appeared and sidled towards them over the polished floor.

"Can I help you, madam?" he asked.

Grandmother stared at him. Then she smiled. "Are you not Dr. Rotimi's son? The one who went to school with my grandson, Sociable? The one who was studying accountancy?" she asked warmly.

The young man looked briefly at her well-worn traditional clothes. He became cold and cross.

"No, madam," he answered. "I am not."

There was a silence. Then Uncle Tunde pointed to Anna Hibiscus and said, "We have come to buy clothes for this child. She is soon to travel overseas and—"

"We are not a children's clothes store," the young man interrupted, and sidled away.

"Let us go," Grandmother said loudly. "This is not a shop for decent, respectful African people."

On the street they all took a deep
breath of the hot, spicy, friendly air, and
Anna Hibiscus took Grandmother's hand.
Grandmother turned towards the next big,
fine, cold shop. But as she turned she saw a
different shop on the other side of the road.
An old, rickety shack of a shop crowded
with plastic buckets and cups and plates,
T-shirts and dresses and rubber shoes, all
in shiny plastic packets. The sign above the
door read:

YOU WANT! WE GET!

The shop trader stood in the doorway, waving her arms and talking loudly to some customers. In front of the shop were tables and chairs and another woman selling cold drinks and frying black-eyed bean fritters.

Grandmother stopped. She looked from the small, hot, rickety shop to the fine, cold ones. She looked down at her hot feet swelling out of her shoes. She made up her mind.

"These oyinbo shops are as cold as their countries," she said. "You young ones carry on. Call me before you buy." Grandmother turned to Anna. "Don't worry, Anna Hibiscus. We will find something nice for you. Go with them," she said.

So Anna Hibiscus, Clarity, Joy, Common Sense and Uncle Tunde left Grandmother sitting at one of the outdoor tables, ordering a cold drink and smelling the acara fritters.

They went from shop to shop. They
stroked the soft materials when the shop
attendants were not looking and gasped at
the printed prices. Common Sense shook
her head. There was nothing their money
could buy.

In the window of the last shop Anna
Hibiscus saw a beautiful red suit. The skirt
was long and full. The jacket had long
sleeves and a big collar. There was even a
hat to match! Common Sense read the price
label and gasped. It was far too costly. Uncle
Tunde could not count that much in his
pocket, or even in his bank.

"Money does not reach."

He sighed.

Anna Hibiscus tried to be brave.

"Don' cry," whispered Clarity. "Is too big anyway."

Common Sense sighed. "There is nothing here for us," she said.

"Let's go and find Grandmother," said Uncle Tunde.

Grandmother was sitting outside **You want! We get!** drinking cold Fanta and talking to the fritter lady and the other customers. She looked at the cousins' faces and Anna's tears and shook her head.

"Sit down-o," she said. "I have a surprise for you."

The shop trader brought out many shiny packages. Inside some were long socks in pink and green. Inside others were cardigans, also in pink and green. There were pink girls' undershirts with frills around the neck and arms.

As Anna Hibiscus's tears dried up, Grandmother and the shop trader started to haggle.

Grandmother demanded happily, "Are you trying to cheat me with that price? I know these clothes have been waiting in your shop to be sold for a long-long time."

Just as happily, the shop trader wailed, "You are trying to rob me! I sent my sister's daughter to an oyinbo shop just now to buy those things for you."

"Nonsense!" shouted Grandmother, enjoying herself. "You want to cheat me! With your prices I will have to send the child cold overseas. Do you want everybody to think we do not know how to dress our children properly?"

"You think I am a fool!" the shop woman argued hotly. "Just because I took pity on your granddaughter and found her some clothes. You think I be one cash madam? I am too poor to put clothes on my own children's backs!"

"Don' vex me!" shrieked Grandmother. "Na me, an old woman trying to clothe her own grandchild!"

Loud and long they haggled happily, until finally they arrived at a price they were both satisfied with. The cousins picked up the parcels, and the shop trader counted Uncle Tunde's money.

"I see you enter dat first shop," she said, "and I shook my head. That Rotimi boy!"

"You are telling me that was Dr. Rotimi's son!" Grandmother demanded.

The shop trader nodded.

Grandmother sucked her teeth. "The chicken that mistakes itself for a peacock forgets to run from the cooking pot!" she said. Standing up, she marched across the road and re-entered the first shop.

After a while she came out smiling. "The chicken realizes its mistake when it is plucked for the pot," she said.

Uncle Tunde and the shop trader laughed and laughed. Grandmother had been plucking the feathers of the young man who had pretended to be too fine to know them. Grandmother had thrown him straight into the cooking pot of her hot-hot anger! She did not like people making a fool of her.

Anna Hibiscus hid behind her big parcel and giggled. The shop assistant had looked like a chicken with his long neck – even though he had acted like a peacock!

At home, Joy laid the pretty cardigans and socks and undershirts on Anna's bed for everybody to admire.

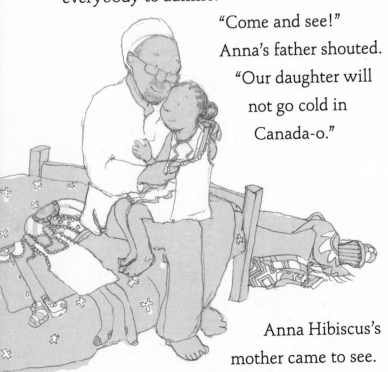

"Come and see!" Anna's father shouted. "Our daughter will not go cold in Canada-o."

Anna Hibiscus's mother came to see. She looked at the thin cotton clothes. She knew she would have to text Granny Canada with a long list of warm woolen coats and sweaters and tights and trousers … and everything!

Anna Hibiscus's mother looked at Grandmother's tired face. She could see Grandmother's swollen feet. She would not let Grandmother know about the text. Oh, no! Anna Hibiscus's mother bent her knee to Grandmother.

"Thank you, Mama," she said. "I am grateful for what you have done for our daughter today."

Grandmother smiled. "Oyinbo shops and countries may be cold … but you, my daughter, you are not!" she said warmly.

Anna Hibiscus looked at them. Some countries were hot, and some countries were cold. Some people were hot, and some people were cold. But she, Anna Hibiscus, was lucky. Her family was – just right!

Good Luck, Anna Hibiscus!

Anna Hibiscus lives in Africa. Amazing Africa. In Africa she was born, and in Africa she has stayed. It is the only place she knows. But soon Anna Hibiscus is going overseas. She is going to visit her granny in Canada. She is going to see snow! Soon Anna will say goodbye to everybody in the big white house. For one whole month she will be in a country covered in snow.

Anna Hibiscus has been waiting and waiting and waiting and waiting to see snow, to touch snow, to taste snow!

One week before she was due to go, Anna Hibiscus was sitting in her favorite mango tree singing her song about snow. Only one more week! Then for a whole month she would see snow, snow, snow! One whole month without her mother and her father, without Grandmother and Grandfather, without all her aunties and her uncles and her cousins. Could she live without them for a month? A whole month without her brothers. She definitely could not live for one whole month without Double Trouble.

Maybe she could get
off the plane, hug Granny
Canada, see snow (and touch it
and taste it), get back on the plane and
come home in time for Christmas with
her own family. She did not need a whole
month to see snow.

Anna Hibiscus needed to talk to
somebody about this. Surely nobody
thought it was a good idea to send her a
million miles over the ocean alone to stay in
the snow for one whole month! She jumped
down from the mango tree and ran into the
big white house.

Inside she found Grandmother bent over photo albums, waving scissors and glue.

Anna ran up to her, but just as she was opening her mouth Grandmother said, "I cannot answer any questions. I do not want to hear about anything. I am busy. Go elsewhere." Anna Hibiscus closed her mouth.

She could hear Grandfather moving about in the next room. Anna Hibiscus opened the door. Grandfather had his head deep in a cupboard looking for something. He moved, and everything in the cupboard fell out. Everything – including Grandfather. He sat on the floor surrounded by a mountain of boxes and bags and old clothes.

"Can I help you, Grandfather?" asked Anna.

"Do I look like I need help?" replied Grandfather crossly.

Anna Hibiscus quietly closed the door. She sighed a big sigh. She could hear the sound of sewing machines coming from the bedrooms. That was strange. Normally the aunties sewed downstairs.

Anna climbed up the stairs, but when she reached the top Miracle and Sweetheart were blocking her way.

"You're not allowed to disturb them, Anna Hibiscus," Miracle said.

"They are all very busy," said Sweetheart.

Anna Hibiscus was cross, and she climbed over them anyway. She could hear the voices of the big cousins coming from the big girls' bedroom.

"I need to talk to you!" shouted Anna Hibiscus, trying to open the door. "What are you doing?"

"We are not doing anything," said Angel, peeping around the door.

"Only homework," said Chocolate.

"For next term," said Clarity.

"You don't have to do it," said Wonderful.

"Because you won't be there," said Benz.

"You can't talk to us now," said Joy.

"Because we are too busy," said Common Sense.

"Go and play," said Thank God.

"Don't bother us any more," said Sociable.

The door shut. Miracle and Sweetheart were looking at her. Anna Hibiscus wanted to cry.

She ran downstairs to Uncle Bizi Sunday.
He was always in the kitchen, and he
always had time for her.

"Don' run here!" shouted
Uncle Bizi Sunday. "Can'
you see I'm busy?"

Tears jumped into
Anna's eyes. It was not
fair. Double and Trouble
were banging pots under
the table. Why was she not
allowed in?

Then she saw her mother sitting
on the veranda, knitting.

"Don't say
anything, Anna
Hibiscus," her mother
said sternly, when
she heard Anna's
footsteps. "I am
counting stitches!"

94

Anna Hibiscus climbed back into the mango tree and let the tears jump out of both her eyes. She had not even gone to Canada yet, and already she had been forgotten by everybody. But her father and the uncles – they would be home later. They would listen to her.

But when the uncles came home they gathered around Uncle Tunde's laptop. Anna tried to talk to Uncle Tunde, but he ignored her.

Anna Hibiscus fell asleep waiting for her father to come home. She did not wake up when he carried her to bed. When she woke in the morning he had already gone back to work. Why was he working so much when it was her last week at home?

All that long week Anna Hibiscus sat alone and lonely in the mango tree. Only Koko the parrot kept her company.

"Koko? Koko?" he asked softly.

"Everybody's forgotten me already," she said, stroking his soft feathers.

"Koko, Koko," he replied. It was all that he could say.

"I love you too," Anna Hibiscus said. That was what she wanted to say to everybody. Not "goodbye" for one whole month, but "I love you" forever. And now nobody would listen, except for Koko.

So Anna Hibiscus said it to him over and over again all week.

"I love you," she said (that was for Grandfather).

"I love you," she said (that was for Grandmother).

"I love you," she said
(for her mother).

"I love you,"
she said (for her father).

"I love you,
I love you,"
she said
(for Double and Trouble).

"I love you," she said for Auntie Joly and
Auntie Grace and Uncle Tunde and Uncle
Bizi Sunday and Uncle Habibi and Clarity
and Common Sense and Joy and Benz and
Wonderful and Chocolate and Angel and
Miracle and Sweetheart and all of her aunties
and uncles and cousins.

"I love you," she said one million times.

Koko rubbed his soft feathers on her wet
face and croaked.

The day before she was going to Canada, Anna Hibiscus heard a voice under the mango tree.

"Annnnaaaaaaaa. Anna Hibiiiiiiiiiiscus," Chocolate sang up. "Grandfather wants to see you."

Anna Hibiscus was silent.

"Anna!" her mother called. "We need you here. Come down!"

Anna Hibiscus did not move.

"Oya, we are all waiting for you," Grandmother called softly.

Anna Hibiscus peeped out from behind the mango leaves. There were her mother and her father standing on the balcony with Double and Trouble. There were Grandmother and Grandfather on the veranda with all of the uncles. Her cousins were leaning out of their bedroom windows, shouting. Uncle Bizi Sunday was hurrying from the kitchen to look for her.

The aunties were gathered at the foot of
the tree, readying themselves to climb up!
When Auntie Joly reached a thin branch—
   Uh-oh! thought Anna. I'd better go down.

Anna Hibiscus followed the aunties into the house. All of her family was smiling at her. Nobody said anything.

Then Grandfather cleared his throat. "We wish you good luck on your journey, Anna Hibiscus," he said.

Uncle Tunde came forward, holding out a brand-new, digital camera!

"This is for you, Anna Hibiscus, from all of your uncles. So that you can take many, many pictures of Canada and show us everything and not forget anything. We ordered it on the Internet on my laptop."

Anna Hibiscus was too surprised to speak.

Grandmother smiled and nodded, and Anna's mother put a soft parcel into Anna's hands.

"Don't open it now, Anna Hibiscus. Save it for your first night in Canada," she said.

"And just in case you get lonely," said her father, holding out an envelope, "you can buy a phone card to call us any time, every day if you like, and especially Christmas Day. Here is the money."

Anna Hibiscus's eyes opened wide to think that she would be able to speak to everybody, even when she was far away in Canada! She wrapped her arms around her father and cried. He had worked long and hard to give her that money. He dried her tears.

Grandmother put a little photo album in
her hands.

"This is so you do not forget
who you or your family
are when you are in a
strange land."

There were
photos of everybody
including Anna
Hibiscus herself.

"Don't cry again,
Anna Hibiscus," said
Common Sense.

"We made something to
cheer you up," said Chocolate.

"Look," said Benz, holding out a book.
It was a big book with the words
GOOD LUCK, ANNA HIBISCUS! written
in giant letters across the front. Anna
Hibiscus opened the book. There were
handwritten stories about Anna selling

oranges and singing in the National
Stadium, with little drawings
of Anna and all
her family. The
cousins had done
it all themselves.
The second half of
the book was blank.

"For you to write down your new
adventures in Canada," said Angel.

"To read out to us," Miracle added.

"When you come home," said Joy.

Anna Hibiscus smiled a huge smile.
"Thank you!" she said.

She could not wait to read her old
adventures to Granny Canada and to write
down her new ones. She was going to take
pictures of snow on her camera to keep forever. She was going to look at photographs
of her family and phone home every day!
Maybe one month was not so long after all.

Anna Hibiscus smiled and smiled.

"Tha's better," said the aunties. "A crying girl cannot wear an outfit like this!"

And they held out a full red skirt, a little red jacket and a little red hat. It was exactly like the outfit Anna Hibiscus had seen in the expensive oyinbo shop. But this one was just her size, and the material had red hibiscus flowers printed all over it and was lined with soft, warm, red cloth ready for the Canada cold.

Anna Hibiscus stretched out her hand to touch it. Her mouth made an O.

"Oya! Come on!" shouted the aunties and uncles and cousins. "Let's see you!"

Anna Hibiscus put on her new outfit. She felt so happy! How could she think that her family had forgotten her?

"Good luck, Anna Hibiscus," said Grandfather. He held out a suitcase. On it were stickers. GB. France. USA. Soviet Union. India. "This was mine when I was a young man," he explained. "It is yours now. Travel safely, my granddaughter."

"But, Grandfather," Anna Hibiscus said. "I did not know you had been overseas."

"I have not," said Grandfather proudly. "I have never traveled. But as a young man I thought of going to look at other places. So I bought a suitcase and collected a few stickers. Now you can take it traveling for me."

"Thank you, Grandfather," Anna said, taking the suitcase. This was an important job she was going to do for Grandfather. And it was only for one month.

"I have something for you too, Anna Hibiscus," said Uncle Bizi Sunday.

And he did. He had pots and pots of Anna's favorite food for the family to enjoy together that night. Rice cooked with tomatoes and onions and a lot of chili peppers. Chicken and yam fried in palm oil and a lot of chili peppers. Bean curd cooked in banana leaves and a lot of chili peppers. Strips of smoked fish in a lot of chili peppers. Goat meat in a tomato and onion stew with garlic and a lot of chili peppers.

"Hot and spicy food to keep out the cold,"
he said.

"Oh, thank you, Uncle Bizi Sunday!"
said Anna gratefully. She had heard about
foreign food from her father, so tonight she
was going to eat a lot. Enough to fill her up
for the whole month. Anna Hibiscus sighed
happily.

Double and Trouble put one last pot onto
the pile. An empty pot.

"Snow!" they shouted.

Everybody clapped and cheered. "Bring
back snow!" they shouted.

Anna Hibiscus was silent. A big lump blocked her throat. Everybody had given her something, and she had done nothing for them.

Just then Koko flew in through the open window. He was tired of waiting for Anna Hibiscus in the mango tree. Over their heads he flew. Then he shouted!

"I love you! I love you! I love you!"

Anna Hibiscus's whole family opened their mouths in astonishment. They laughed and cried and clapped their hands. Anna Hibiscus's mouth made a very big O. Koko was shouting in her voice!

"I love you! I love you! I love you!"

"I LOVE YOU!

Anna Hibiscus had done something for her family after all. Love. It was the most important thing in the world.

I LOVE YOU! I LOVE YOU!"

Atinuke was born in Nigeria and spent her childhood in both Africa and the UK. She works as a traditional oral storyteller in schools and theaters all over the world. Atinuke lives on a mountain overlooking the sea in West Wales. She supports the charity SOS Children's Villages.

Lauren Tobia lives in Southville, Bristol. She shares her tiny house with her husband and their two yappy Jack Russell terriers. When Lauren is not drawing, she can be found drinking tea on her allotment.